MARVEL
SPIDER-MAN

MARVEL READING PROGRAM

W9-AKU-896

**Book 1
short -a**

A NEW MAN

© 2018 MARVEL. All rights reserved.

All rights reserved. Published by Scholastic Inc., *Publishers since 1920*. SCHOLASTIC and associated logos are trademarks and/or registered trademarks of Scholastic Inc.

The publisher does not have any control over and does not assume any responsibility for author or third-party websites or their content.

No part of this publication may be reproduced, stored in a retrieval system, or transmitted in any form or by any means, electronic, mechanical, photocopying, recording, or otherwise, without written permission of the publisher. For information regarding permission, write to Scholastic Inc., Attention: Permissions Department, 557 Broadway, New York, NY 10012.

This book is a work of fiction. Names, characters, places, and incidents are either the product of the author's imagination or are used fictitiously, and any resemblance to actual persons, living or dead, business establishments, events, or locales is entirely coincidental.

ISBN 978-1-338-27205-5
Printed in Jiaxing, China 68
First printing 2018

SCHOLASTIC INC.

Peter Parker **has class**.
He carries a **backpack**.

His **class** goes
to a **lab**.

A spider **lands**
on his **hand**!
It bites.

Peter hangs
from walls.

His **hands** shoot webs!

He is Spider-Man!

A **bad man grabs cash.**

Peter stops the **man**.

Peter is a new **man**!